Sheep in a Shop

P9-DHK-584

Nancy Shaw

Sheep in a Shop

Illustrated by Margot Apple

Houghton Mifflin Company Boston

Also by Nancy Shaw and illustrated by Margot Apple:

Sheep in a Jeep
Sheep on a Ship
Sheep Out to Eat
Sheep Take a Hike

Text copyright © 1991 by Nancy Shaw
Illustrations copyright © 1991 by Margot Apple

All rights reserved. For information about permission to
reproduce selections from this book, write to Permissions,
Houghton Mifflin Company, 215 Park Avenue South,
New York, New York 10003.

Library of Congress Cataloging-in-Publication Data

Shaw, Nancy (Nancy E.)
 Sheep in a Shop/Nancy Shaw; illustrated by Margot Apple.
  p.   cm.
 Summary: Sheep hunt for a birthday present and make havoc of
the shop, only to discover they haven't the money to pay for things.
  RNF ISBN 0-395-53681-2   PAP ISBN 0-395-70672-6
 {1. Sheep — Fiction. 2. Shopping — Fiction. 3. Stories in rhyme.}
I. Apple, Margot, ill. II. Title.
PZ8.3.S5334Shm   1991   90-4139
{E} — dc20   CIP
                                    AC

Printed in the United States of America

WOZ   30 29 28 27 26 25 24 23

To Fred, for suggesting a birthday theme, to Scott, for sharing many happy birthdays, and to my parents, for making birthdays possible.

—N.S.

For these sheep-loving shopkeepers: Anne; Barbara & Art; Claire, David & Diana; Cree, Ann & Marcia; Jan; Janet; Leslie & Maude; Linda; Mark; Michael; Nancy.

—M.A.

A birthday's coming! Hip hooray!

Five sheep shop for the big, big day.

LUNCH
ICE CREAM

COUNTRY STORE

SALE

9

Sheep find rackets. Sheep find rockets.

Sheep find jackets full of pockets.

Sheep find blocks.

Sheep wind clocks.

12

Sheep try trains. Sheep fly planes.

Sheep decide to buy a beach ball.

Sheep prefer an out-of-reach ball.

Sheep climb. Sheep grumble.

Sheep reach. Sheep fumble.

Sheep sprawl.

Boxes tumble.

Boxes fall in one big jumble.

Sheep put back the beach ball stack.

They choose some ribbon
from the rack.

They dump their bank. Pennies clank.

There's not enough to buy this stuff.

Sheep blink. Sheep think.

What can they swap to pay the shop?

Sheep clip wool, three bags full.

Sheep trade.

The bill is paid.

Sheep hop home in the warm spring sun.

They're ready for some birthday fun.